i

Dark Valley

Don Allen

ISBN: 979-8-9932322-3-2

eISBN: 979-8-9932322-4-9

Publisher: Don Allen

Also, by Don Allen

1 8 AM

I was at my desk by eight, which was somewhat unusual for me. Normally, my duties had me chasing bad guys in the early morning hours, but recently it's been relatively quiet in Arizona, at least on the crime front.

I'm James Barlow, a sheriff on the Governor's task force. I've been with the state's sheriff's office for, what is it now, ten years. Prior to that, I served three years in the military, then attended Arizona State University on the GI Bill, earning a degree in police sciences with a minor in criminal justice. After graduating, I joined the Phoenix Police Department. After two years, the sheriff's department recruited me. Solving a high-profile murder case put me on their radar. My part last year in the recovery of the kidnap victim, Susan Dillingham, Arizona's 3rd District Congressional Representative, landed me in my current assignment on the Governor's task force.

I'm not a big guy, only five foot seven, weighing in at 177 lbs, and I can almost press my weight, but not quite. On the positive side, I have black belts in several of the martial arts. If permitted, I'd just as soon replace my department-issued 9mm

Glock, in my mind an overrated piece of hardware, for my personal sidearm, a 1911 Colt 45. If you want to stop a bad guy fueled by fentanyl, you need to make a big hole.

***

I was in early this morning for a meeting that Bud Rouster had called. Bud is the head of the task force, a 22-year veteran of the sheriff's office. "Get your coffee," Bud called out. "Grab a seat and let me have your attention."

After a few crude remarks, we were all seated around the conference table. There were five of us. I was the junior member.

"Gentlemen, the feds have noticed a small uptick in the drug traffic here in Arizona. This past month, they've interdicted several shipments coming over from Morelia. The feds believe the shipments are coming from the Santo Domingo Hacienda, home of the Ortega Cartel, one of the newer drug cartels. The smugglers use old, often forgotten, off-road trails. We believe their destination is the Gila River Indian Reservation."

"The Governor is embarrassed that the feds are catching these criminals while *we sit on our hands*, to use his words. I want you out there! Contact your sources, and let's get some results. Otherwise, this task force may be history!"

As we were breaking, Bud called out, "James, stay for a bit, I need to speak with you."

"Oh shit, what did I do now? Park in his space?"

"James, thanks for staying. I have a special assignment for you. The Governor of New Mexico, Charlie Maxwell, has requested our help, you specifically. Your notoriety in the recovery of the Congresswoman caught his attention. The son of one of Albuquerque's leading families has gone missing. The father, López Gonzalez, is the Chancellor of the University of New Mexico. The son, Rafael Gonzalez. He's fifteen and has not been seen for three days. The parents are worried sick."

"And what am I supposed to do? They have a very capable police force. I've met a couple of their people at FBI-sponsored seminars."

"I understand," said Bud, "but our Governor, in his wisdom, told Governor Maxwell he'd help, and your name came up. You should plan to be away for two or three days. I don't want you turning this into a vacation. Good luck."

I headed home to pack an overnight bag and to tell my wife I would probably miss our 17th wedding anniversary.

"What do you mean you're going to Albuquerque for a few days?" Mary explodes when I tell her. "We have reservations at that new French restaurant. Not an easy thing to get."

Mary and I were married when I was an E-4 in the army. She has always supported me, and I her, in her academic career. Progressing through the academic credentialing system, she earned her PhD in literature and was now a tenured professor on the Tempe Campus. She is a recognized expert on 19th-century authors.

"You can thank our good Governor the next time you vote. He's the one who volunteered me to find this kid."

2 Albuquerque

Albuquerque is a six-hour drive from Phoenix, so I decided to fly. Getting to the airport, sitting in the waiting area, flight time, counting time on the taxiway, waiting to take off, and getting a rental car took close to five hours. So, I saved an hour and got a rental that reeked of cigarette smoke. 'I'll drive next time,' I told myself.

I found the Public Safety Headquarters on Roma Avenue, between 4th and 5th. I was told to ask for Captain Bigalow. He was heading up the Gonzalez investigation. I did so. The desk sergeant asked me to have a seat while he called upstairs for an escort. About thirty minutes later, a young lady came to collect me.

"James Barlow? We've been expecting you. Please come with me, Captain Bigalow is waiting." This was said as if I were a perp.

She takes me to the third-floor conference room, where the Captain is waiting with three of his men. All four greet me with frozen faces.

"Sheriff Barlow, have a seat," Bigalow says, pointing to one in the middle of the table.

He then gives me his welcoming speech. "I don't know why you are here other than our Governor wants you on the case. Apparently, you got his attention last year. So, given that, welcome to Albuquerque."

"We've prepared a synopsis of the case to date; it's in the folder in front of you. Please don't take the folder from this room; the press would have a field day if they got their hands on it. Look through it while we take a short break. We'll reconvene in thirty minutes. There's coffee on the credenza," he said, pointing to the back wall as he and his people filed out of the room.

Talk about a cool reception. I skipped the coffee; it was probably laced with a laxative. I started reading the Gonzalez file.

Rafael Gonzalez, age 15, was reported missing on Tuesday afternoon. He had not returned from school. He attended the Mission Achievement and Success Charter School, an elite school for Albuquerque's gifted.

A missing person case was not opened until the next day, after an extensive search was conducted of probable places he could be.

It was discovered that two of his school buddies were also missing. Their families did not receive the same initial attention as the Gonzalez family.

Jimmy Crow, age 17, was Navajo; his family lived on the Canoncito Indian Reservation. Jimmy boarded at the school and had access to an old Dodge Caravan. He used the vehicle to go home on weekends.

Alex Clive, age 16, attended the school through a special scholarship program for disadvantaged students. He had an impressive juvenile record.

Interviews had been conducted with family members. No useful information was obtained.

Jimmy Crow's sister, Sandie Dove, claimed Jimmy often boasted he could disappear for months, living off the land just as his ancestors did.

This initiated an extensive aerial search of a 50-mile radius of the city.

Extensive interviews were conducted with all family members. Other than that provided by Sandie Dove, there were no leads.

The State Police were on the lookout for Jimmy's minivan, but there were no sightings.

The FBI had been contacted, alerting them to a possible kidnapping and transport of a minor across state lines. For the time being, they were treating this as a local matter.

Captain Bigalow and his men returned an hour later; no apologies for the delay.

"Well, Sheriff Barlow, any thoughts?"

"No. It appears you have everything covered."

"Thank you," he said with some disdain.

I got the sense he really did not want me involved.

7

"When will you be returning to Phoenix," said more as a statement than a question.

3 Sandie Dove

The following morning, I was still thawing out from yesterday's chilly reception. I'd be damned if I'd cave to Bigalow's desire to have me out of his hair. I checked out of the motel and, in my cigarette-reeking rental, headed west to the Canoncito Indian Reservation.

The Canoncito Indian Reservation was a stand-alone piece of the Navajo Nation. The Nation straddles New Mexico, Arizona, and Utah with a few detached pieces.

The previous year, Navajo youths dressed as warriors had attacked and destroyed the Lake Powell Data Center. The Center's construction was shrouded in corruption and was located on Navajo ancestral burial land. The surviving security video footage showed young men covered in war paint, making them unrecognizable. But there was one I recognized, more by his demeanor than by facial recognition. My cousin Billy Eagle. He was my mother's sister's youngest son.

9

My grandfather was Johnathan Harris. He served with the 3rd Army during WWII. Later, using the GI Bill, he earned a law degree and hung his shingle in Flagstaff. While defending an Indian on an assault charge, a totally bogus charge by the way, witnesses testified that the two drunks attacked the Indian youth. The charges were dropped. Johnathan was invited to the reservation to celebrate, where he met Aiyana, my grandmother. They had two daughters, my mother, Bluebird, and her sister, White Dove.

Both daughters attended the University of Arizona. Bluebird earned a teaching certificate, and White Dove an RN license. At the University, Bluebird met my father, George Barlow.

White Dove returned to the reservation to work at the Indian medical clinic. In time, she became a Nurse Practitioner, and the clinic became known as White Dove's Women's Clinic. She met and married a local doctor, Ben Richards, known to the tribe as Burning Tree. Together, they had three sons and a daughter. Billy Eagle was the youngest.

Genetically, I'm one-quarter Navajo, enough to make me a voting member in the Navajo Nation.

My goal this morning was to talk with Sandie Dove. I knew she knew more about Jimmy Crow than she was letting on. I found the To'Hajiilee Navajo Center. Sandie Dove's family home was on Blue Moon Lane.

Going up to the house, a young woman was just coming out. *"Are you Sandie Dove?"* I asked in Navajo.

Looking somewhat surprised to hear a white man speaking Navajo, she said nothing. A middle-aged woman, her mother, I assumed, stepped out of the house, "What do you want, I thought we answered all your questions."

In Navajo, I introduced myself. It turned out she knew of White Doves Women's Clinic. I was invited in and offered tea.

"Thank you for speaking with me. I know the Albuquerque police were here. I've met them, a bunch of assholes, please excuse my language."

Mother and daughter laughed at that. *"Yes,"* they agreed.

I then asked them to tell me what they could, explaining that one of the missing boys was from an influential family and that the search would only intensify. The mother could add no more, but the daughter looked as though she was holding something back. I didn't press.

As I got up to leave, I took out one of my cards and jotted down White Doves' cell number on the back. *"If you think of anything that you think would be useful, please call me at this number, or if you prefer, call the Women's Center and White Dove will pass it on to me."*

4 Dark Valley

Several days before my arrival in Albuquerque, the three boys decided to start their summer break early. It was Alex's idea, but the other two eagerly agreed.

"Well, what should we do?" asked Raf. "I have some money, Jimmy has a car, and Alex has, well, he has what he has. I know, let's take a road trip."

"No, if we just take off, they will be looking for my car. I know, let's go to my grandfather's cabin," said Jimmy. "We can hang out and drink beer."

"Right, you two won't be able to stand up after one beer," scoffs Alex. "Where is this cabin?"

"It's in the Gila National Forest, a place called the Dark Valley."

"Cheerful sounding place," said Raf.

"No, it's a very nice place," said Jimmy defensively. "The name refers to an Apache massacre of Navajo in the 1800s."

"When I was young, my grandfather took my father and me there on hunting trips. After his death, my father and I continued the tradition. Since my father's passing two years ago, I haven't been back. Now would be a good time to go."

It was agreed. The three boys, instead of going to school on Tuesday morning, headed south in Alex's car. No one was missed other than being listed as absent on the school attendance record. It wasn't until Raf didn't return home that night that there was any concern, and a missing person case was opened the next day, Wednesday.

It is over a two-hundred-mile drive to Dark Valley. The valley itself straddles the New Mexico-Arizona state line and is located just north of Whiterocks Mountain. Along the way, they bought some canned food, chips, and other essentials. Alex tried to buy beer. His fake driver's license was rejected by the store clerk, an old woman who probably was there when New Mexico became a state.

Navigating the last ten miles on off-road tracks took close to an hour. It was late afternoon when they found the cabin.

Jimmy was the first to enter. It was just as he and his father left it three years ago, some dust, but otherwise all neat and tidy. It took three tries to prime the pump; they were getting concerned they'd have no water.

"What now?" Raf asked.

"We cook the steaks we bought at the last stop, and I was able to score a six-pack at the service station back in Albuquerque," Alex said, popping open a warm beer.

"In the morning, let's take a hike down to Bloody Lake. There is some fishing gear in the closet. I think there are still three rods there."

5 Tech Boys

Dan Holuk and Nick Norton, two of the top academic performers in the Electrical Engineering Department at the University of Colorado, were working on a new weapon. Needless to say, given the woke campus environment, they kept their work secret. The only person privy to it was their adviser, nicknamed 'The Colonel,' who was the titular head of the ROTC unit at Bolder. Dr. Borman was a valued professor at the University, having received several patents in laser technology after a distinguished career in the army.

Once their gadget was perfected, the two approached Dr. Borman, asking how they best proceed.

"Well, I don't think this is something that you're going to sell on Amazon. If you commercialize it, the ATF will be on your case. One of my former deputies now commands a small, little-known unit at Holloman AFB in New Mexico. It's an army research facility that studies new technology; some say Star Wars weapons. I suggest you visit him. I'll call him if you like."

15

Three days later, Dan and Nick arrived at the Air Force Base. When asked where they were going by the guard at the front gate, they said they had an appointment with Colonel McElroy at the Army's Small Arms Research Facility.

They were directed to park in the visitor space while the airman at the visitor center took their information. "This is an Air Force Base," the airman snickered.

"Cut the crap, Jones. You know there's a army contingent on base," said the desk sergeant. "You have to excuse him, he's new here. Now what can I do for you?"

After several phone calls, he said, "There is no Small Arms Research Facility on this base. Is there anyone you can contact?"

Nick, now getting agitated at the bureaucracy, called Dr. Borman. Borman tells them to sit tight; he'll call McElroy.

An hour later, Colonel McElroy arrives at the Visitors' Center and signs the two in. He explains the Small Arms Research Facility is a 'hush-hush' operation on the outskirts of the base. Since it was getting late, he suggested the two get a room at one of the nearby motels. He recommends the Holiday Inn in Alamogordo. He will meet them at the Visitors Center in the morning. He then calls his aide, Major Dickerson, to adjust his schedule for the following day and to have the tech team on hand to evaluate a new weapon.

The two find the Holiday Inn. It's in a small commercial center about ten miles from the base's main gate. Nick wants to bring their 'project' into their room, but Dan insists on leaving it in the trunk of the car. "It will be safe there," and he didn't want to draw attention to it. Nick finally agrees; he's not eager to lug it through the lobby.

They get a good dinner at the steakhouse across the street. They are in bed by ten.

About three a.m., Nick is awakened by concerns about the 'project' and decides to check on it. As he approaches his car, he sees two men attempting to break into it. He shouts and runs toward them. The one closest pulls a pistol and shoots. The two, grabbing Nick's keys, make off with the car.

The desk clerk hears the gunfire, and she calls the local police. Amidst the swirling blue lights, Nick is found dead in the parking lot. By this time, Dan is outside frantically trying to find out what has happened. The detective in charge of the crime scene takes Dan back into the hotel's lobby and, in a quiet corner, gets what information he can.

Dan is distraught and has trouble staying focused. He is able to provide basic information on the car, year, and model, but not the plate number. It is registered to Nick. He also alludes to a secret project in the trunk that they were to demonstrate later that day at the Small Arms Research Facility on Holloman AFB. He gives them Colonel McElroy's phone number.

6 Bloody Lake

The three boys were up early the next morning. Jimmy had the stove going; his father had left a supply of kindling and wood for the stove after their last visit to the cabin. Alex took charge of preparing breakfast, eggs, and toast. Raf filled the old tin coffee pot with water from the kitchen pump.

As they were finishing up, Jimmy was encouraging them to move along. "We should get down to the lake, the fish here bite early."

Taking the fishing gear, Jimmy led the way down to Bloody Lake. It was a 15-20 minute walk through the forest. If there was a path, Raf and Alex didn't see it.

Arriving at a secluded lakefront beach, Jimmy's two companions ask how the lake got its name.

"I don't know, I've always known it as Bloody Lake. Perhaps some frustrated fishermen called it a Bloody Lake in exasperation."

"We need some bait," Raf said.

Jimmy went over to a dead tree, and taking his knife, lifted off a piece of bark. Beneath were a dozen or so big white slugs. "Use these," he said, "better than worms."

Soon, the three had their hooks baited and in the water. After a while, Raf complains, "Where are the fish?" Alix is reclining against a large boulder, half asleep.

They all perk up when they hear a vehicle, no, make that two vehicles, pulling up in the adjacent cove. Due to the vegetation, they can't see the cars. Jimmy slips to the top of the hill and looks down. There are two cars. One is being driven into the bushes under a large pine. Raf and Alax have joined him, and Alax motions for them to be quiet.

The man who had driven the first car into the bushes reemerges and is heard to say, "We can leave it there for a few days. No one will find it."

"They better well bloody not," said the man stepping out from the second car. "If you hadn't shot that guy, we could have delivered the car, been paid, and been on our way. But no, you had to shoot."

"Stop f…..g complaining. We'll bring Boris here tomorrow; he can get the stuff out of the car, pay us, and we will all be happy."

The two get in the second car and drive back up the trail.

The three boys sit there wondering what to do.

It's not a puzzle to Alex. He's up and headed for the hidden car. The other two reluctantly follow.

"What are you doing?" yells Raf, "they might come back."

"Not today, you heard them say they'd be back tomorrow. Let's see what's in the car."

They find the car. It's well hidden in the bushes.

"It's locked," said Jimmy as Alex jimmies open the driver's door with the 10" Bowie knife he found in the cabin.

They found nothing of interest in the car other than some candy bars, which they took. Alex walks around to the trunk. "How are you going to open that?" asks Raf.

Taking his knife, Alex tells Raf to find him a large stone. With the knife point inserted into the keyhole, Alex hits the hilt of the knife a few times, and the trunk lid pops open.

"Where did you learn to do that?" asks an amazed Raf.

"Summer school."

In the trunk, there is a strange-looking backpack. It has a gauge on the flap and a long hose coming out of its side with an attachment on the end. There is also a rifle. Well, it looked like a rifle, maybe a Buck Rogers Rifle. Lying under the pack is a three-ring notebook containing a manual. There is also a small solar panel.

Looking around, Jimmy says, "Let's get this stuff back to the cabin and figure it out."

7 Buck Rogers Rifle

Back in the cabin, Raf starts with the manual. "Don't play with it until I figure out how it works!!" he yells as the other two are horsing around with the 'rifle.'

Shortly, he announces, "This is some kind of laser weapon. Hook that tube to the butt of the gun," he directs them.

There is a soft pinging from the backpack. Alex, holding the gun, squeezes the trigger. There is a blinding flash and a painful crack as the weapon fires. A small hole, about an inch in diameter, appears in the side of the cabin.

"Holy shit!!," Alex cries as he drops it.

"This is no toy," said Raf as he collected the gun and, with the backpack over his shoulder, the three stepped out onto the porch.

Raf, a reasonably good marksman, aims at a branch a hundred yards away. He fires, hits the branch at its juncture with the tree. It falls to the ground.

He tries another shot. There is only a clicking sound.

"You broke it," Alex says.

"No, the manual said it's only good for seven or eight shots before needing to be recharged. That's what the solar panel is for. The sun is too low; we'll tackle it in the morning."

The next day, following Raf's directions, they set up the solar panel and connect it to the backpack. "The manual says it takes six hours of direct sunlight to recharge the unit. Or only thirty minutes if we could plug it into a wall socket."

"That's not going to happen here," said Jimmy.

The three boys are sitting on the porch, admiring their handiwork, when they hear two gunshots in the distance.

"The lake?"

They follow Jimmy's nonexistent trail back to Bloody Lake. As they get close, they crouch down and slip through the bushes back to where they first saw the cars.

There is no one there. It's quiet. Then Jimmy points to the two bodies lying by the water.

8 The Theft

The previous night, the two car thieves were holed up in a seedy motel on the outskirts of Las Cruces. The older one is still berating the other about needlessly shooting the man in the parking lot.

"He was getting too close. He could have identified me," the younger one said for the umpteenth time. "Let it go. It's done. What time is Boris getting here?"

"He'll be here first thing in the morning. He's going to want whatever is in the trunk of that car. That's what he paid us for."

The following morning, the younger one is nervously explaining to Boris why he shot the guy.

"Where is the car now?" scowls Boris.

"We hid it in the Gila National Forest, just off Rt. 180. We can get there in two hours."

"Two hours!" roars Boris. "Get in my car, we're going there now."

Boris was calming down until he was directed off the main road and onto a small dirt road leading into the woods. He almost lost it when the younger man said it would be another thirty minutes of iffy dirt roads before they'd get to Bloody Lake.

They finally crested a small hill, and the lake was laid out before them. "Beautiful," said Boris. "Looks like a good place to leave two bodies."

The two thieves look at each other as Boris smiles. "Just kidding."

They arrived at the spot where the car was hidden.

"Well, go get it," snaps Boris.

The two walk over to the car, and one is about to unlock the trunk when they see the keyhole has been punched out and the trunk lid is askew. The younger one desperately looks around as the older one searches the car.

"Boris, there is nothing here. Are you sure they had it in the car?"

Boris was sure. He had listened in on the police channel as details of the murder were radioed in. His army contact confirmed that Dan Holuk was adamant that the prototype weapon was in the trunk of the car.

"Someone has been here," said the younger man. "They broke into the car and stole whatever it is you're looking for."

"You bumbling idiots," screamed Boris as he produced a pistol and shot, first the younger man point-blank, and then the older thief as he turned to run. The two bodies were left lying by the water.

When he got back on Rt. 180, where there was cell-tower coverage, he called his army informant. "We've got a problem; my two idiots lost the item. .... No, I don't know what we do next. Just sit tight and let's see what develops."

9 Boris

Boris was a former Soviet intelligence agent. After the fall of the Soviet Union, he worked for a time as a Russian agent. When payment for services became a sticking point, he branched out. Now in his late 60s, he wanted a retirement nest egg, so he took on tasks for whoever paid – paid up front.

Through a Chinese student placed at the University of Colorado, the People's Republic of China heard rumors of a prototype field laser weapon being designed for the infantry. Although unconfirmed, the PRC's primary intelligence organization, the Joint Staff Department of the Central Military Commission, sought more information and, if possible, the prototype. Boris accepted a contract, half a million dollars for the technical details and another half million for the prototype. A quarter million was paid as a retainer. He was on the hook to produce.

Boris was put in contact with the student, a Chinese intelligence agent. Together, they had Dan and Nick under loose

27

surveillance when they learned that Dr. Borman had arranged for the two to visit an army research facility at Holloman AFB that studied Star Wars weapons technology.

Boris was racking his brain with how to proceed when he remembered an army lieutenant he'd met in Germany years earlier. The lieutenant liked the ladies, liked booze, and liked to gamble. The makings of a good security leak.

Boris kept track of this potential asset and had used him a few times over the years. If the money was right, he always produced. This asset was stationed at Holloman AFB.

He made the call. At first, he said no and hung up on Boris. Boris's second call, after a bit of research, began with a reminder that the asset had a $100,000 outstanding balance at the *Giddy Up* Casino in Las Vegas, and that the casino was about to dispatch a collection team. Borris promised to pay the debt if he would just pass on information about Holuk and Norton's visit to Holloman.

10 Home

After seeing the bodies on the lake shore, the three boys made a beeline back to the cabin, put their stuff in Jimmy's car, and left.

"What the hell do we do now?" Raf asked no one in particular.

Jimmy took charge. "The first thing we are going to do is call the State Police and report the bodies." Seeing the look of disbelief on the other two faces, he added, "Anonymously."

"We need a story," said Alax.

"I know," said Raf, "we visited the Grand Canyon. We just wanted to get away before the end of the school year. What about the laser gun?"

"I'll hide it on the reservation – but you two can't mention it."

Jimmy dropped the two off at the school and then headed home to the reservation.

***

Rafael called his Dad's cell phone number. "Hay, Dad, can I get a ride home?"

"Where the hell have you been, Rafael? Your mother is worried sick."

"I forgot to call her in the excitement. Three of us decided to take a short trip to the Grand Canyon before school let out. We just up and left on Tuesday after school. I thought I'd be back before I was missed."

That night, after a regal dressing down, Rafael was restricted to the house for the summer.

***

Alex took the city bus home. His mother asked where he had been.

"Three of us decided to take a short trip to the Grand Canyon before school let out," he answered.

"That's nice," she said and continued, fixing dinner, no further questions.

His father wasn't aware he had been missing for the past few days.

***

Sandie Dove was the first to see Jimmy when he got home. "You've had the family worried. There was an Arizona Sheriff here asking about you. Where were you?"

"Raf, Alex, and I decided to take a short trip to the Grand Canyon before school let out."

"Bullshit," she snapped. "You went to grandfather's cabin!" Do you realize that if anything happened to the *bilagáan*[1] boy, you would have been blamed?"

---

[1] Bilagáana is the traditional Navajo word often used to refer to non-Indigenous people—especially those of European descent.

11 Murder

Earlier that day, the central office of the New Mexico State Police received an anonymous call reporting two bodies. The lady manning the emergency line turned to her supervisor, "I think we have a crank call here. Some kid reporting two bodies by *Bloody Lake*. Where is this lake? I've never heard of it. Should I send this to the Sargent?"

"Bloody Lake is in the Gila National Forest, and yes, send the report upstairs. At the worst, it's just a prank call, you will be razzed for a few days. If it's for real and you sit on it, you'll be fired."

When Sargent Hoyt got the report, he called out, "Lieutenant, we have a report of two bodies by Bloody Lake. It's probably a bogus call, but we should dispatch a team to check it out."

"What are the details?" asks the Lieutenant.

"Two bodies lying on the beach on the south side of the lake. There is also an abandoned car. This is in the Gila National Forest. No other details."

The Lieutenant consults a map and tells the sergeant to call the Milan State Police Barracks; they appear to be the closest to Bloody Lake.

The day shift at the Milan Barracks is thrilled to be called out on a probable murder. "Another f.....g wild goose chase snaps one senior trooper."

Given the remote location, they decide to take one of the Barracks' older SUVs. "No loss if we damage it," quips one of the youngest of the three men dispatched.

Following faded traces of possible roads, the three make it to the lake by early afternoon. There are no bodies to be seen.

"Follow those tire tracks around the edge of the lake," one of them suggests.

Ten minutes later, "Hold up, I think I see a body up there."

The SUV creeps forward; two bodies become visible, both lying beside the lake as reported.

"Stop here," the team leader says. "We don't want to drive over any tracks."

Looking around, he sees a car hidden in the bushes, doors and trunk open. He gets out of the vehicle and, from a distance, takes some photos on his cell phone, which he sends back to his

33

sergeant and a copy to the State Police Headquarters in Albuquerque.

Almost in unison, they respond: 'tape off the crime scene and don't touch anything.'

From headquarters, the message is longer. 'We are flying in a forensic team by helicopter. Need to find a good landing area. You may be required to collect the team and their gear. Sit tight.'

An hour later, the first responders are told to meet the helicopter in a meadow three miles east. Two of the three remain to guard the crime scene while the team leader goes to pick up the forensic team.

By the time he and the forensic team are back on site, three more vehicles have arrived from other barracks with food, tents, and a generator. It's going to be an all-night affair.

Due to temperature fluctuations, the initial estimate of time of death was sometime between 24 and 36 hours ago. The two were shot with what looks like a small-caliber pistol, perhaps a 9mm, at close range.

The forensic team dusted the car for prints and found that a half dozen or so different hands had touched it. It was going to take some time to sort out whose prints. One of the techs observes, "The one thing for certain, this is the car that was stolen at the Holiday Inn murder scene in Alamogordo. Are these murders connected?"

12 The Three

Over the next couple of days, the police forensic lab in Albuquerque is able to identify several of the fingerprints. Two are from the dead bodies found at the lake. Another two are linked to Dan Holuk and Nick Norton.

Sheila Carvalho, the newest member of the department, is puzzling over one set of prints. "Oscar, last week, three boys were reported missing; one was Alex Clive. The prints from his 'juvi record' match some of our unknown prints."

Oscar comes over and double-checks.

"Interesting, they match. I wonder how they got there?"

He knows his friend, Captain Bigalow, was assigned to the Rafael Gonzalez missing person case. His first call is to Bigalow.

"William, I've got an interesting tidbit for you. Your three missing kids ... yes, I know they are home now, but we just found fingerprints of one of them on the abandoned car at the

Bloody Lake murder site ... yes, for sure. Alex Clive. There is also one other set of prints we have not identified – one of the other two kids, perhaps?"

***

Captain Bigalow dispatches two of his men to find Alex and question him. They find him at home, alone, playing a video game. He refuses to talk to them. They take him into custody and take him downtown.

Alex is totally uncooperative, forcing the officers to carry him into the station, which was caught on cellphone video. He's allowed to make a phone call; he calls his mother. An hour later, Mom arrives with the family lawyer in tow. Mom, having a son with previous run-ins with the law and a husband who cycles through the local jail, has an attorney on retainer, her brother, a locally noted defense attorney.

Due to the way Alex was taken into custody, the videotape, and the attempted questioning of a minor without parental consent, Captain Bigalow is forced to release Alex with the pending prospect of a civil lawsuit.

The first thing Alex does when he gets home is call Raf. "The police were at my place this morning. We left fingerprints on the car. They are trying to tie us to the murder of those two."

"Shit, I think I touched the car too," said Raf.

As Raf was saying those words, Captain Bigalow dispatched two teams to obtain fingerprints: Jimmy Crow's and Rafael Gonzalez's.

***

Jimmy Crow was expected to be found at his sister's home on the Canoncito Indian Reservation. The two officers find Jimmy's home. His Mother claimed he's not there. Her daughter, Sandie Dove, asked what they wanted.

"We need his fingerprints," the older officer said. "We think he's involved with the two bodies we found at Bloody Lake."

"And what authority do you have here?" bristles Sandie. "You're not with the tribal police. You're not federal. You're trespassing on the reservation, a sovereign Nation."

As the two leave, Sandie yells out, "Jimmy, get your sorry ass down here. What are you involved with? What happened at granddad's cabin?"

His sister can be as mean as hell when she's riled up, and she's riled now! He tells her everything – except about the Buck Rogers gun. He has it hidden in the back of his car.

"That Arizona Sheriff, Barlow, I think his name was, said you'd end up being blamed. I'm taking you to Uncle Nakai's farm, and then I'm visiting White Dove.

"Oh, come on," whined Jimmy, "Uncle Nakai's farm is in the middle of nowhere. And who is this White Dove?"

"His farm is in Many Farms, in the Navajo Nation; it's in Arizona. As for White Dove, she's a respected Indian healer and one of the two women on the council of elders. If you stay here, you will become the white man's scapegoat."

***

As the two officers are being turned aside by Sandie Dove, two others are headed to the home of López Gonzalez, located adjacent to the University of New Mexico. They have called ahead, so they are expected.

Invited into the home by Dr. Gonzalez and his wife, the lead officer explains, "Dr. Gonzalez, we are glad your son is home, but there are some questions. You may have read about the bodies found at Bloody Lake. There was also an abandoned car. We recovered several sets of fingerprints from the car. We've traced one set to Alex Clive, one of your son's companions. We are still looking for the owner of another set of prints. Would it be possible to get Rafael's?"

The Chancellor is now the color of a beet. "Rafael," he bellows, get down here. "Tell the officers your cock 'n bull story about going to the Grand Canyon."

Rafael tries to keep up the pretense, but his voice is soon trailing off when he realizes no one believes him.

The lead officer reports the police's findings about the fingerprints. Rafael knows the other set of prints is his. He melts down, and the whole story comes out, including the Buck Rodgers Rifle.

13　Colonel McElroy

Captain Bigalow is intrigued by the Buck Rodgers Rifle.

"Is this a piece of fantasy?" he asks no one in particular. "The three boys are obviously tied to the car theft at Hellman AFB last week. I think we need to talk with the friend of the murdered victim, Dan Holuk."

The Captain decides to call this Holuk fellow himself.

"Mr. Holuk, this is Captain Bigalow. I'm with the Albuquerque police department. I think we may have a lead on your missing rifle, but first, let me offer my condolences for the loss of your friend."

After a bit more talk, Dan agrees to come up to Albuquerque. He'll be there in the morning.

Late morning, Holuk arrives; Colonel McElroy and his aide, Major Dickerson, are with him. They find the captain's office, and after introducing themselves and declining coffee, Colonel

McElroy states the purpose of his presence – "The country's interest in the new weapon."

Captain Bigalow, against department protocol, has his team lay out what the police have so far.

"The two men who killed Nick Norton and stole his car were found along with the car. The two car thieves are dead. Their bodies and the stolen car were recovered at Bloody Lake in Gila National Park. We've accounted for all fingerprints found on the car."

"We've tied three boys from the Albuquerque area to the site. One of the boys, the one whose fingerprints were found on the car, is a delinquent; been in and out of the courts. The second boy, an Indian, Jimmy Crow, refuses to give us his fingerprints. Or, more accurately, his sister refuses to let us have access to him. We think the unidentified prints are his."

"Now, on a more positive note, the third boy, Rafael Gonzalez, made a full confession. He said the three of them were playing hooky and planned to spend the week at the Indian boy's family cabin. They heard some gunshots and, upon investigation, found the two bodies ... and the car. The delinquent broke into it. They found what he describes as a Buck Rogers Rifle in the trunk. The Indian took it."

"Returning home, the Indian placed an anonymous call to the State Police to report the bodies. He then had Rafael promise not to tell anyone about the weekend end, especially about the rifle."

"Now it's my belief," continued Bigalow, "that this was a kidnapping that got derailed. The delinquent and the Indian talked the Gonzalez kid into going with them. His father is the Chancellor of the University of New Mexico. In another day or so, they would have called the father and demanded money for Rafael's return. After the father dropped the money off at a dead drop, the three boys would return as if nothing had happened. But the bodies ruined their plans."

"An interesting theory," said the Colonel, "but the missing rifle is a prototype using new laser technology. I've requested it be classified as secret for the time being. What that means is the FBI will be taking over this case."

"What, you can't do that!" snaps Bigalow.

"It's been done. FBI agents are on their way here to gather the case files; files on the car theft and associated murder, the bodies at Bloody Lake, and the files on the three boys."

"Major Dickerson, get the information on Jimmy Crow. We need to find him!"

14 Flight

"I'm taking you to Uncle Nakai's in Arizona, get packed." They were on the road thirty minutes after the two deputies left.

Jimmy put his stuff in the back of his sister's car. On the bottom, he had a backpack and one of his father's old canvas gun cases.

"You're taking Dad's rifle?" Sandie asked.

"I might go hunting for rabbits."

They needed to cross state land separating the Canoncito Indian Reservation from the main body of the Navajo Nation. It's a short ride, but Sandie wanted it behind them before the State Police could be in position to watch for them. It was a safe bet that Jimmy would be wanted by the authorities within the next few hours.

It's a two-hundred-mile drive to Many Farms, Arizona. Many Farms is one of the smaller farming communities in the Navajo Nation. They arrived as the sun was setting. Uncle

Nakai is surprised to see them. Sandie explains why they are there and that Jimmy needs a place to stay for a week or two.

"Of course he can stay here," Nakai says, "but this can't be the long-term solution."

"No, I'm going to talk to council members tomorrow to see what they can do. If nothing is done, Jimmy will be railroaded."

The next morning, Sandie Dove was retracing her trip back to Window Rock, a mid-sized Indian town abutting the New Mexico State line, where the Navajo Nation's administrative offices were located. She had an appointment with White Dove at the Department of Health.

"Where can I find Ms. Richards?" she asked the young receptionist.

"You can find her office on the second floor, ma'am."

Skipping the elevator, Sandie Dove rushed up the stairs, found the door with Mrs. Richards, Head of the Nation's Women's Health Program. She knocked and then entered.

White Dove, hearing a person in her outer office, called out, "Can I help you?"

"Yes. I'm Sandie Dove. I called you earlier. Your nephew, James Barlow, told me to contact you if we needed help."

"James told me you might call. Come in and talk to me."

Sandie entered and sat in the chair that White Dove pointed to.

As Sandie started to tell Jimmy's story, White Dove stopped her, "Please call me White Dove; Mrs. Richards is too formal."

Sandie resumed her narration, finishing with her fear that her brother was being made a scapegoat.

"My nephew expected as much. After you called last night, I called him. He will be here in time to join us for lunch. You can give him all the details then."

"Where is Jimmy now? No, don't tell me I don't need to know," White Dove said.

About then, White Dove's cell phone chirped, "That's James, he just arrived at the Cactus Pit," she said.

The Cactus Pit was about a quarter mile up the street. They walked as White Dove described the Cactus Pit. It was a 50s café that had been rehabbed and was now the go-to eatery for local office workers.

I had secured a booth and waved them over when they entered.

"I thought I'd be seeing you again." "The police, Captain Bigalow in particular, are buffoons, but dangerous buffoons. When I met with them, I had the feeling they were ready to pin Rafael Gonzalez's disappearance on an Indian, any Indian. Jimmy fit the bill. So, tell me what is going on, what made you call White Dove?"

45

Sandie let it all out, the police visit asking for fingerprints, and recent news about bodies being found at Bloody Lake. The lake near her grandfather's cabin. Her fear was that Jimmy would be implicated in the murders.

I took it all in. At the end, I asked White Dove if Bud Evans, Indian name Great Bear, was still head of the Reservation's police force. "I need to see him."

15 Reinstatement

Bud Evans was now the head of the Public Safety Division. He had me by a few years, but as a kid, he was the big dog among the kids. In my younger years, I spent many summers with my grandmother's family on the reservation. When visiting, I was called Little Fox and was Great Bear's shadow. Today I was going to call in some childhood favors.

The Public Safety Division was a stone's throw from where we were. I asked my aunt to take Sandie back to her office. I'd join them in a bit.

I found the Public Safety Division building. It was an upgraded police station. Entering, I asked to see Chief Evans.

"Is he expecting you?" the desk sergeant asked.

"No."

"The Chief is tied up, won't be available later today. If you leave your name, I'll let him know you were here."

Shaking my head, I was thinking, 'The Nation had succumbed to white men's bureaucracy.'

"Tell him Little Fox needs to see him – now!"

As the desk sergeant started to bristle, I flipped open my Arizona Sheriff's credentials. He stopped in mid-sentence, picked the phone up, and called the Chief's office.

"Go through those doors, you'll find his office at the end of the hall. And with that, he buzzed the doors open."

Entering his outer lobby, I found him there waiting for me.

"Great Bear, it's been years since I've seen you. I see you made it to the top. Congratulations."

"And you, Little Fox, you're an Arizona Sheriff. I didn't realize they lowered their standards," he said with a chuckle.

After a few minutes reliving the past, he asks, "I know you're not here for a social visit. What do you need?"

"I need to be reinstated as a Navajo Deputy Sheriff. If you recall, I was sworn in many years ago to help solve a cattle-rustling case that was rampant here in the Southwest. I believe I'm still one of your inactive deputies."

"If you don't mind me asking, why?"

Taking the coffee he had offered earlier and settling onto the couch, I told him about Jimmy and the facts as I knew them. "The New Mexico police will probably make him the scapegoat for the whole mess and end up charging him with murder."

48

"And what makes you think he's not guilty?"

"Gut feeling – and I've met Captain Bigalow. He's the kind of guy who would indict his mother if it helped his career."

"Ok, Little Fox, I'll see what I can do. Come back in an hour. I'll have your badge and credentials waiting for you at the front desk."

In that hour, I called Bud Rouster in Phoenix. "Bud," I started, I needed to pull him into this slowly, "remember that special assignment you gave me to assist the police in New Mexico? Well, it's gotten a bit more complicated." I then gave him a quick rundown of the case. "I've requested the Reservation police to reactivate my tribal Deputy Sheriff's standing so I can operate on the Reservation ... yes, I think it's necessary. I'll keep you posted. Suggest you change my status to *temporary assignment* with the Navajo Nation ... Thanks."

16 Break-in

I insisted on seeing Jimmy before I did anything else. Sandie yielded. We headed for Many Farms, leaving her car at the Window Rock police parking lot. The drive gave us time to talk, but she could not add much more than I already knew.

She talked about Jimmy's earlier years. His relationship with his father and grandfather. Those relationships were good, but his relationship with his mother was a little rocky. She was too demanding.

Uncle Nakai was surprised to see Sandie Dove back so soon, and more so by her being accompanied by a Deputy Sheriff.

"Where can we find Jimmy?" she asked after the initial introduction was made.

"He's in the barn tending the horses," Uncle Nakai said, pointing to the barn.

"You wait here," she told me. "I'll get him."

A few minutes later, she returned with Jimmy. A small boy for a seventeen-year-old. He looked like he was ready to bolt, but Sandie had him by his arm.

"Nakai, where can we talk with Jimmy – privately?"

Getting the message, he pointed to a bench in a shaded portion of his yard, "Over there, I have some chores to do in the house."

As Sandie and Jimmy settled on the bench, I found an old chair; we all sat staring at each other.

"Okay, Jimmy, let me tell you what I know." I spent the next few minutes reciting what I knew. It didn't take long; I didn't know much. I finished with my observation, "They want to tie you to the murders."

Jimmy was nervous but not on the point of panic.

What was I missing?

We talked a bit more, but he would add nothing else to the story. I suggested he stay put, and I would see what could be done. Sandie and I left after she had a few words with her Uncle.

As we drove down the dirt farm road, she said, "I asked him to call if Jimmy left."

We picked her car up and drove in tandem, headed back to the To'Hajiilee Navajo Center and her home on Blue Moon Lane.

***

The Navajo Police had the street blocked off. Her mother was in the street yelling at a paramedic who was loading a man into the ambulance.

We parked the cars and walked into the chaos. My Navajo Deputy Sheriff badge got us past the officer securing the perimeter, got Sandie to her mother, and me to the officer who appeared to be in charge.

Identifying myself, I asked what had happened.

"There was a break-in. The house was ransacked. Walls torn out. Someone was seriously looking for something. The neighbor heard the noise and finally came over to investigate. The intruders fled, shooting him, leaving him in the street bleeding. The paramedics tell me it doesn't look good."

"Any idea what they were looking for?"

"No."

About then, the neighbor on the other side came forward with her 6-year-old son. "He saw them," she said.

"What did you see?" the officer and I asked almost in unison.

Three bad-looking men, the boy said. The one who shot Mr. Night Owl looked like Boris."

"Boris?" we both said, puzzled.

"Yes, like the Boris on *Rocky and Bullwinkle*."

The officer said, "My kids watch *Rocky and Bullwinkle* every afternoon. Boris is a small bald guy with a pencil-type mustache." And smiling to himself, muttered, "And Natasha was probably driving the getaway car."

17 The Rifle

As Sandy Dove and her mother were walking through their house, the mother kept saying, "Why, why did they do this?"

Staying back, I kept thinking, 'Jimmy's not telling us everything.'

The two women were trying to straighten up one of the rooms when more company arrived: Captain Bigalow of the Albuquerque Police Department and an Army Colonel.

Walking over to them, thinking, 'What the hell do they want?'

Grinning, he starts, "Barlow, what the hell are you doing here? This isn't Arizona. Are you lost?"

I let him run on for a bit and then, pulling out my new credentials, asked, "Why are you on the reservation? I thought your people were told they, and you by extension, aren't welcome here."

He was startled for a moment before an older man stepped forward, flashing an FBI badge, "Deputy, there have been some new developments, and the Bureau has been called in. Let's talk in private."

By now, Bigalow was smiling ear to ear, knowing the FBI did have legal standing on the reservation. And based on my recent experience with the FBI, I was wondering what kind of incompetent fool I had here.

"Deputy, I'm Agent Parnell, and I am aware of your recent experience with the *Tweedle Dum and Tweedle Dee* team, as you described them, and who, by the way, have been reassigned to clerical duties in the Hoover Building pending their retirement. Hopefully, we can work this out together."

Agent Parnell appeared to be a seasoned agent, probably in his late 40s. "We'll see," I responded, "but that doesn't explain why you are here now."

"No, it doesn't. Let's let Captain Bigalow explain," he said as he waved the other two over and motioned for the Captain to talk to me.

Grudgingly, he started, "We interviewed Rafael Gonzalez again yesterday, somewhat more forcefully. He cracked and confirmed the three boys had planned their absence. There was no kidnapping. The second day at the cabin, they found a car in the bushes by the lake. One of them, Alax, broke into it. There was nothing in the car worth noting. He popped the hood of the

55

trunk, where they found what Rafael described as a Buck Rogers Rifle. They took it. Back at the cabin, Jimmy took charge of it after they fired it a few times."

Looking at the Colonel, he went on, "The next morning, they heard gunshots. Investigating, they found the two bodies, dead, by the lake. All the car doors and the trunk lid were open, as if someone was looking for something, maybe a Buck Rogers Rifle," he said with a smirk.

"The three packed up and hightailed it home. On the way, Jimmy insisted on making an anonymous call to the State Police to report the two bodies."

"Jimmy kept the rifle, making each boy promise not to mention it."

"Having Rafael's statement, we called Dan Holuk to confirm what was in the trunk. He, Colonel McElroy, and an FBI agent were in my office the following morning, insisting on finding Jimmy Crow – ASAP."

Colonel McElroy added, "If this so-called rifle is what Dan claims it is, it's a major step forward in small arms development. I've requested that it be classified as top secret until it's fully evaluated. That is why the FBI is involved."

"I'm guessing that is what they were looking for when they broke into the house earlier today," I said. "I would also guess that they are the ones who killed the two car thieves who muffed the job."

Going on, I asked, "Who knew all this?" I asked Bigalow.

"Only two of my deputies, Colonel McElroy and his aide, and Dan Holuk."

"Well, it appears someone leaked."

"Who broke into the house?" Agent Parnell asked.

"The neighbors saw three men," I said. "A neighbor, Mr. Night Owl, went out to confront them. He was shot. He's now in the hospital, in critical condition. A neighbor's 6-year-old son claims the man who shot Mr. Night Owl looked like Boris, the Boris in *Rocky and Bullwinkle.* A small bald guy with a pencil-type mustache."

Bigalow looks at me as if I'd been nibbling peyote and starts to say something when Parnell cuts him off, "That's a better description than we usually get. Sometimes kids see more than we give them credit for."

They spent another quarter hour trying to make sense out of what they were just told, and a few follow-up questions. Then they were gone.

18 Reality

"What's Jimmy's cell number?"

Sandie gave me the number; I called. It went to voicemail. I called again. And a third time. Finally, Jimmy answers,

"Whoever you are, you're persistent," was his greeting.

This is Sheriff Barlow. "Your mother's home was ransacked. Her neighbor was shot. Any idea why?"

He was silent, finally, "Is my Mom okay?"

"Yes. You can talk to her in a moment, but first, where is the Buck Rodgers Rifle? The Albuquerque police were here this morning. Rafael Gonzalez talked. Claimed you had the rifle. The FBI and an Army Colonel were also here. They are very interested in getting it back."

More silence on his end.

"Look, I told your sister I would try to keep you out of this. I'll come to you tomorrow to pick up the rifle, and you can stay in hiding."

I handed my cell phone to Sandie. She and her mother spent the next ten minutes talking with Jimmy, reassuring him they were fine.

Getting my phone back, I told Sandie I was going to Many Farms in the morning. She insisted on coming with me. I said "No."

"You need me. Uncle Nakai shoots first, then asks who it is later."

I finally relented. I would like Dan Holuk, the rifle's inventor, to come with us to verify it's his rifle. I called Agent Parnell to give him an update and to get Dan's number, and of course, he insisted on joining my growing entourage.

I got hold of Dan and told him I thought I had located his rifle. "I'd like you to come with us tomorrow. I need someone to identify the weapon." He agreed.

"Can you meet us at Sandie Dove's home, about 8 a.m.? ... Here are the directions. Dan, now this is important, don't tell anyone where you are going. There has been one leak resulting in someone ransacking Sandie's home looking for the rifle."

19   The Leak

That evening, "Boris, I got news for you. I've found the rifle. Jimmy Crow, as we suspected, has it."

"Where the f... is he?" snarled Boris. "That's what I'm paying you for."

"He's at his Uncle's farm in Arizona."

"And where is this farm?"

"It's in the Navajo Nation. That Sheriff from Arizona and Sandie Dove are driving up there tomorrow, and they are taking Dan Holuk with them."

"And how does that help me?"

"Ya. I see your point. The best I can suggest is to have your people follow them."

"Brilliant," yells Boris.

As the call disconnects, Boris thinks, 'There must be an Indian census or some genealogical source that links these people together.'

He calls an old Cold War contact, a sleeper living in Alexandria, Virginia. He's in his late 80's. At one time, Mikhail maintained an extensive information network that could locate anyone in North America.

It took Boris some time to locate Mikhail. He was living in a retirement home in Northern Virginia, *The Woods* or *The Woodlands*, some place like that. It was going on 3 a.m. on the East Coast; he'd call in a few hours.

Early the next morning, Mikhail's time, Boris got Mikhail on the line.

"Mikhail, Boris here. ... Boris who? Your old friend. Remember how we set up that politician to take the fall for spying? He got us some good stuff."

"Oh, now I remember you. That was a fun time."

"Look, I need a favor. Do you still have access to your information sources? ... Yes, I know you're retired, but maybe you could point me in the right direction." Boris then went on to describe what he needed.

Mikhail suggested Boris access the Navajo Peoples Database. "It's a secure database, but here is how you can access it." Boris eagerly jotted down the directions Mikhail provided.

"Mikhail, thanks, you're a lifesaver. Enjoy your ice cream social."

Boris was soon in the Navajo Peoples Database. He quickly found Jimmy Crow and Sandie Dove, their mother and her brother, Nakai. The database showed he lived in Many Farms, Arizona, on Eagle Nest Road. A search of Google Maps located the small community, and an enlarged view showed a ranch house and some outbuildings at Nakai's address.

Sitting back satisfied with himself, he next called Michael, one of his people.

"Michael, I got a new assignment for you and Johnny." He gave them the details and directions to the farm. He finished up with an admonishment, "Don't screw this up as you did at Bloody Lake or the more recent fiasco at the Canoncito Indian Reservation."

Michael started to point out that it was Boris who shot the people, but Boris disconnected when he was in mid-sentence.

20 Race To The Farm

It was getting close to eight thirty when Dan arrived. So much for an early start.

Agent Parnell was there at seven. He insisted we use his Chevy Suburban; it was larger, and he had his gear, or more accurately, his arsenal in it. Sandie sat in front with Parnell and provided directions. Dan and I had the back, where we catnapped.

"What kind of place iss Many Farms?" Parnell asked Sandie.

"It's in the high desert, enough groundwater to support a half dozen horse ranches, not farms. I guess at one time there were farms, but not now, just ranches," said Sandie. "The Indian ponies they breed are in demand by mounted police around the country. Uncle Nakai is the exception. He raises hay to feed the horses. It's a very small community."

***

Michael and Johnny left Albuquerque around eight a.m. In their white Ford Econoline van. "We need a new ride," complained Johnny, "this rust bucket is an antique."

"Quit complaining, it works, no one notices it," retorted Michael.

"I know, just park it on the side of the road, and people will think it died there. By the way, where is Boris? He usually comes along just to tell us what to do – and then he shoots them."

"Boris has a meeting today. I overheard him talking with a potential new customer. Some dude from Pakistan who wants to get his hands on the F-35 weapons systems. Apparently, the Paki's are concerned about a conflict with India. His s son attends the University of New Mexico; the visit provides him cover and cannot be rescheduled."

"I'm surprised he trusts us," said Johnny.

"He doesn't, but he has no choice. I'm to call him periodically. Probably should call him now to let him know we're on the road."

***

As Parnell's SUV speeds along I-40, it passes an old Econoline van. At Gallup, they get off I-40 and head north. Parnell's foot is too heavy on the gas. He's pulled over for speeding by the New Mexico State Police. He flashed his FBI badge, giving the trooper an earful about being stopped in the middle of nowhere.

The trooper doesn't give a fig about the FBI and threatens to take Parnell in if he doesn't stuff a sock in it.

From the back seat, I identify myself to the trooper as a Navajo Deputy Sheriff and tell Parnell to cool it, accept the ticket, and we'll be on our way.

As all this is transpiring, a white Econoline van passes.

Just south of Many Farms, we pass another white Ford Econoline.

"Damn, those vans are common around here," mutters Parnell.

As we drive up the long dirt trail to Nakai's spread, Nakai's old lab runs down to greet us. Parnell parks beside an old farm truck. Nakai ambles out to greet us. *"What are you doing back so soon?"* he asks in Navajo, *"and who are these two?"* he says, pointing to Parnell and Dan.

Sandie walks over, gives him a hug, and explains what's going on, finishing with, *"Where is Jimmy?"*

"I think he is in the barn cleaning up after the livestock." About then, a white Ford Econoline van is coming up the trail to the farm, in a cloud of dust. It parks in the middle of the yard. Two men get out. The older of the two comes over and starts asking directions, claiming to be lost. He wants to find the town center.

As he distracts us, the younger man slips around the side of the vehicle, comes up behind Sandie, and grabs her. One arm around her neck and a pistol to her head.

The older man drops his 'a-shucks' veneer, "Where is Jimmy? My buddy will shoot the girl in the leg if I don't get an answer by the time I get to ten. He starts a slow count. One ... two ... three... "

21 Interrogation

Jimmy's in the barn. He's fiddling with the Buck Rogers Rifle. He's had the backpack charging for the past day and is now connecting the hose to the rifle's butt. He sees the SUV drive up. He's close enough to hear his Uncle and Sandie. He's about to come out when the white van arrives. He sees and hears his sister being threatened. The man with the pistol to her head is about to shoot her.

Yesterday, Jimmy had the rifle out, firing it over in the next valley. It was a damn sight more accurate than his old hunting rifle. He targets the man with the gun. He's confident he can take him out and not hit his sister. He fires.

There is a loud clap like thunder, a flash, and a small hole appears in the man's forehead, and a fine red mist sprays from the back of his head. The shot continues into the van, hitting the fuel pump. A small engine fire starts, which quickly turns into a major conflagration.

Amidst the confusion, I sprinted forward and tackled the older man before he could draw his gun. Panell was two steps behind me. Our uninvited guest was soon in handcuffs. Sandie was white as a ghost, Dan was fixed to the spot, unable to move, and Nakai was furious. He rushed over and gave his visitor a sharp right hook to the jaw. I had to pull him off.

Jimmy came out of the barn. He had the rifle and backpack with him. Dan took it, caressing it as if it were a long-lost lover.

After we had all calmed down, to the extent we could, Parnell started to question the man.

"Who are you?"

"How did you find us here?"

"Who do you work for?"

Questioning went on for 20-30 minutes. The man said nothing.

"We should take him out to the *Truth Tree*," Nakai said.

"The *Truth Tree*?" Parnell and I said almost in unison.

"Yes, bring our friend," he said as he headed out into the field.

Looking over his shoulder, he yelled to Sandie, "Tell my old lady to bring some sweet tea out to us. No ice."

There was an old tree in the middle of the field. As we got there, he told Parnell to put our visitor's back up against the tree and handcuff his arms behind the tree.

"James, you got your cuffs with you? I need another pair to reach around the tree."

I gave him my cuffs. The visitor was secured as Nakai directed.

His wife and Sandie soon appeared with a pitcher of very sweet tea; she knew its purpose.

Nakai took it and pored it over our visitor's head, making sure a good portion went down his back. He saved a third to pour down the inside of the man's pants. As it leaked around his shoes, it looked like he had an 'accident.'

"Now what?" I asked.

"We wait. It won't be long," Nakai said with a big grin.

Soon, the visitor started to twitch. The twitching got worse.

Nakai pointed to the ground. There was a trail of red fire ants going up the tree and some up the inside of the man's pant leg. They were after the sugar in the tea. The more the visitor squirmed, the more agitated the little critters became.

"Won't be long now," he said. "Ain't seen anyone last more 'n ten or fifteen minutes with those little fellows nibbling."

The man was soon screaming in pain. Thrashing around like a madman.

Calmly, Nakai asked, "You ready to answer their questions?"

"F… you!!"

Nakai turned to us, "The missus should have lunch laid out for us by now. We can leave him here for the time being."

As we turn to leave, the man, now out of breath from screaming, is whimpering, "I'll talk -- I'll talk."

We remove the cuffs, as Nakai is saying, "Take him back to the barn and dump him in the horse trough. We need to get the ants off him."

Michael talked, and talked -- answering all of Parnell's questions.

He told us where Boris was living and who he claimed to be working for. This month, the Chinese, last year, the Turks, and he has a deal cooking with North Korea. "He has someone at Holloman AFB feeding him information. He is like a sing-song girl in a Saigon Bar – whoever has money," said Michael. "

"Okay, Michael, here is what you are going to do. Call Boris, tell him you have the gun. You and Johnny are on your way back to Albuquerque. You should be there by midnight. If I hear anything funny, you're going back to the Truth Tree."

As Michael was making his call, I called the reservation police. Parnell and I wanted our guest out of the way, behind bars.

Two officers arrived thirty minutes later to take Michael into custody. He started yelling we had tortured him. "Tied me to a tree and let fire ants attack me."

One of the officers looked at Nakai, "I assume he fell in that ant hill over yonder when he tried to run."

Nakai nodded as he continued to chew on the piece of straw.

22 Spy's Den

Parnell made good time getting back to Albuquerque. We were there by eleven that evening.

Boris's address was a townhouse on the outskirts of the city. No lights were on. We tried the door; it was locked, as were the windows on the ground level. Parnell suggested I check the street for Boris's car. When I got back, the front door was open. "It was unlocked after all," he said as he was sliding something back into his pocket.

Entering the house, we saw nothing unusual. I found a cell phone on the kitchen counter. I called Parnell over. Using a piece of toweling paper, he powered it up. The screen lit up, displaying a hand with the middle finger prominently raised. After flipping through it, he said, "There is nothing on the phone; it's new, fresh from the Apple Store."

We made a quick search of the house. It soon became apparent that no one lived there. There wasn't even toilet paper in the bathrooms.

"Michael warned him off," fumed Parnell.

"I doubt anything he told us was true," I said, "except for the part about having a contact at Holloman AFB. He seemed to know what we knew before we knew it."

"Who knew Dan and Nick had a prototype weapon? Who suggested that they stay at a motel close to the base?"

"Colonel McElroy and Major Dickerson," answered Parnell. "And they also knew Rafael fingered Jimmy as having the weapon."

"What's the chance of having the Bureau do a background check on them?" I asked

"Ya, right, I just call my boss and ask him to run a background check on two possible perps, and by the way, they are both army officers assigned to a highly confidential program."

"I see your point. So, what do we do?"

"I'll ask my boss to issue a wanted poster for Boris. Given we don't have a photo of him, I'll suggest we use the cartoon caricature," Parnell snapped.

We both stopped and then laughed at the prospect of a Boris Wanted Poster in Post Offices.

"One thing I can do," Parnell said, "is to request a financial search for any monetary transactions tied to Boris. I'm sure Michael wasn't working for nothing. I'll ask they start with him and then follow the money trail."

"I'll call Captain Bigalow in the morning and have him alert the State Police to be on the lookout for Boris – and Natasha," he added under his breath.

23   Surprise Assignment

"Welcome back, Barlow. Did you enjoy your vacation?"

"It was your idea, Chief; you sent me to Albuquerque. The kids showed up, but then I got sidetracked with a murder and a secret weapon."

"Secret weapon," scoffed Bud. "You are going to tell me the Navajo now have a sonic arrow?"

"Get real Chief, you know that is only a rumor. No, but one of the braves has a rifle that shoots lightning bolts," I said with a straight face, as I turned to get coffee, and then sat down at the conference table.

Chief Bud Rouster had called another of his all-hands meetings. "Gentlemen," he started: this was never a good start.

"When we last met, I told you our Governor is embarrassed that the feds are continuing to catch drug smugglers in our backyard. He's been told that the Department of Homeland Security, that's DHS to those of you who only read the comic strip, is mounting a joint operation with Mexican officials. The target is the Ortega Cartel. Their base of operations is the Santo Domingo Hacienda in Morelia."

"Mexican officials asked that DHS go along as observers. We are to have a beefed-up presence on the border to assist the Border Patrol, and DHS wants one of our people on their assault team to coordinate with our people at the border. Someone who speaks Spanish and is familiar with northern Mexico."

"Barlow, as I recall, you have a friend in the Federales, and you speak Spanish."

"Juan Castro, a Lieutenant with the Federales. We have worked a few cross-border cases together. As for being fluent in Spanish, I get along on the street but would not claim to be fluent."

"Good," said the Chief, "you're our volunteer. The DHS folks are getting together in the morning at the Air National Guard Base. Be there by eight."

My wife was less than thrilled when I told her I'd be away again, supporting some DHS wild-west adventure.

Mary is a tenured professor on the Tempe Campus and a recognized expert on 19th-century authors. "James, you know I'll be in Seattle next week, giving a talk on Jane Austen. But you'd best be home by the weekend. I've rescheduled our 17th wedding anniversary reservation."

I stopped at McDonald's for an egg sandwich and a large coffee on the way to the National Guard Base. The base was wedged in between Sky Harbor International Airport and the FedEx regional shipping center. The guard at the gate waved me through as he pointed to a small warehouse on the edge of the compound, "The feds are in there."

I found a parking space amidst several out-of-state cars.

Entering the building, I found ten or so federal agents. One, a big man, maybe 240 pounds, no fat, the color of ebony, a bald head that was made up for by a large handlebar mustache, came over and introduced himself. "I'm Agent Thompson, the team calls me Leroy. You must be James Barlow. Your Chief said you were tight with the Federales. Have a seat, we're just reviewing our plans for tomorrow."

Settling into the one vacant chair, Leroy then went around the table introducing the team members. Two were former Marine snipers, another a demolition expert, and Charlie was the radio man. Or should I say woman? She was a shapely brunette in her early 30s. The remaining men provided the muscle, each worthy of a spot on any NFL team's line.

"Okay, where was I?" said Leroy.

"Our entry point," said Charlie.

"Yes. We will cross into Mexico at Sasabe, a small border town, at three tomorrow morning. The Mexican Federal Police will meet us there."

"Remember, this is their operation; we were invited in to observe and provide backup if needed. And note the 'if needed' part. We will stand back, keeping our fingers off the triggers."

"What about transportation?" asked one of the linemen.

"The Border Patrol will have three vehicles for us," said Leroy.

"James, you'll ride with the Federal Police if possible and stay in touch with us by radio."

"Charlie, do you have James's radio?

"Yes. I just got six new COBRA walkie-talkies. James gets one, I get one, you get one. "Who gets the other three?"

"Give two to our snipers and the last one to Max, he's heading up the entry team."

"Any questions?" asked Leroy. "If not, get some rest, at two tomorrow morning, an Army Chinook will take us to Sasabe."

24 Santo Domingo Hacienda

The Chinook landed at Sasabe at three. The Border Patrol had three old Chevy Suburbans waiting for us. We transfer our gear and cross the border.

There are fifty or so Mexican Police waiting for us. Their leader approaches, a scowl on his face, "You must be Agent Thompson. I see there are ten of you. I didn't want you here, but my boss told me to let you tag along. You'll keep your men in the back; you're just observing!"

Our people just rolled their eyes. We started getting back into our vehicles when a voice called out, "James." It was Lieutenant Juan Castro.

"James, what are you doing here?" Castro asks.

"You got me. Sounds like your Colonel would rather we not be here."

"Colonel Santiago is an ass. He will more likely as not, screw up this operation. Come, ride with me."

I told Thompson I was going with Lieutenant Castro. He gave me a thumbs-up, noting that part of his plan remained intact.

The group dithered for the next hour as Colonel Santiago inspected his men.

The Santo Domingo Hacienda was about an hour's drive, on back roads, from the border. We got there just as the sun was coming up.

Castro was fuming. "We should have gotten here in the dark. Santiago's delays cost us an hour."

Santiago deployed his four squads in an ark covering the front entrance to the Hacienda. Agent Thompson was told to keep the Americans back in the valley.

Lt. Castro was watching as I told Tompson what was going on and how Santiago deployed his men.

"He what!" yelled Tompson, "No one on the backside of the compound? Ask your friend to hold his squad back in reserve. I'm going to move our people around to the back of the compound."

Castro's English was not that great, but he understood the gist of what Tompson was telling me. "We'll hold here," he said and radioed Santiago to tell him he was holding his men in reserve. Santiago agreed, "Yes, that's a good idea."

The first squad of Federales approached the main gate, demanding entry. Several men were cut down by gunfire. The other two squads started indiscriminately firing at any movement they saw in the compound as they retreated.

In the meantime, Tompson moved his small force up the valley and positioned them behind the compound. When the gunfire erupted, he infiltrated his people into the compound from the back.

The two snipers took out the cartel sharpshooters on the front wall. The explosive expert placed a satchel charge in the generator shed; it exploded, and the Hacienda went dark.

As Tompson made his way into the back of the main house through the kitchen, his team encountered two middle-aged men in a hurry to leave. They were quickly secured with zip ties.

Resistance was eliminated, but Santiago's men were by then in full retreat.

"James, where are you?" my walkie-talkie snapped.

"Still holding as you asked."

"If you can, have your friend bring his men up to help us secure this place – and I need a translator. What can you make of this gibberish?" he said as his two prisoners were protesting their capture.

"Agent Thompson, record what they are saying!! It's important, I'll translate later."

Castro had seven men. He had them advance slowly into the compound. There were a half dozen bodies lying in the dirt by the entrance. Tompson was bringing his detainees out. When he saw me, he called out, "James, get over here. I need to know what these men are saying."

Juan Castro and I looked down on the two who were now on the ground, each with a rifle barrel in their back.

"James, ask them who they are."

They started with a stream of Spanish, far too fast for me to understand. Castro, standing beside me, was listening. He flared up and struck the older man who was running his mouth.

Looking at him, "What was that all about?" I asked.

He claims Colonel Santiago was paid to make this raid fail.

I relayed this back to Agent Tompson.

In my broken Spanish, I asked the two who they were, and what was this about bribing Santiago.

Turning to Agent Thompson, their story is, "The small guy is the number two man in the Ortega Cartel. Manuel Rodriguez, the cartel boss, is not here. He claims that Manuel paid the Colonel $10,000 to ensure this raid failed."

As the Colonel and a half dozen of his men came back into the compound, Santiago started yelling in broken English. "I told you to keep the …" He was cut off by Lt. Castro, who ordered his men to take the Colonel into custody. A few of the Colonel's men started to raise their rifles in his defense, but Tompson, in a deep voice that resonated around the compound and was clear in any language, said, "Don't."

Tompson suggested that Lt. Castro take charge and should order that the Hacienda be searched.

Castro agreed. He and two of his men entered the building. I joined the search. In an upstairs closet, I found a small man trying to disappear into the cleaning supplies. It was Boris. *'How the hell did he get here?'*

Looking at him, he might have been five feet tall – with shoes. With his fat head and pencil mustache, he did look like the cartoon character.

I used my zip ties and then, with Boris in tow, went to find Juan. I explained my interest in the small man. "Juan, I need to ask you a favor, a big favor. Hold on to this guy for two days, then deliver him to me at the Sasabe border crossing. Can you do that?"

Pondering my request for a moment, he agreed, "This is going to cost you, you know."

"Not to worry, this will put you on the FBI's Christmas list."

25 Handoff

Two days later, Parnell and I were at the Sasabe border crossing, swapping stories with the border guards as we waited for Juan and his prisoner. I had called Parnell earlier to tell him I had found Boris. Our conversation was something like the following.

"And you left him in Mexico?"

"That's why I'm calling. He'll be delivered in two days. Do you want to join me when I collect him?"

Not only did he want, but he also insisted on using an FBI helicopter.

Using text messages, I coordinated the handover with Juan. It was scheduled to occur at ten, Wednesday morning. Parnell and I were at the boarder check point at nine.

As the minute hand approached the top of the clock, a Mexican squad car was parking on the Mexican side. Juan got out and was walking toward us as his driver retrieved a small man, handcuffed, from the back of the car. Parnell and I met him in no man's land between the two customs stations.

"Agent Parnell, this is Lieutenant Juan Castro. He is an officer in the Mexican Federal Police Force. Juan, this is Agent Parnell. He is a senior agent with the FBI."

With introductions over, Parnell took the lead. "Lieutenant, thank you for delivering this man. He's a wanted fugitive, responsible for at least three murders. He is also part of a spy network. Who knows he's here?"

"Only a couple of my trusted men. We kept him in isolation in a local jail, away from the other men we picked up. The fallout from Colonel Santiago's arrest helped distract any notice of him."

"As for the Colonel, senior authorities wanted to ignore the bribery charge, bad PR, but because of DHS involvement, they couldn't bury Santiago's duplicity."

"Lieutenant Castro, if there is ever anything I can do for you, call me," Parnell said as he handed him his card with his contact information.

One of Parnell's men switched Boris's handcuffs to his own, returning the original to Lieutenant Castro. The four of us made our way back to the helicopter, Parnell getting into the co-pilot's seat and Boris in the back, squeezed between the other agent and me.

It was a short flight to Fort Huachuca where the FBI had a small holding facility on the base. At the airfield, we were met by a small shuttle bus with two armed guards. At the holding facility, Boris was placed in an interview room and left to 'stew' for a couple of hours while Parnell and I sat in the cafeteria having a light lunch.

"I requested a financial search for monetary transactions tied to Boris, starting with payments to Michael. We have a man at Quantico who is a wizard in tracking money trails."

"Sydney Trocheck," I said.

"Yes, how do you know him?"

"He helped us to unravel the Susan Dillingham kidnapping."

"Okay, anyway, he is a wizard," said Parnell. "Payments to Michael were traced back to a holding company, a company controlled by Boris. He then followed money trails to other recipients. He has quite a nice little network of informers. We will be rolling them up after we determine how Boris used them. One recipient is at Holloman AFB."

After we bused our trays, we headed back to the interview room, where we found Boris in a highly agitated state.

"Well, Boris, what can you tell us?" asked Pernell.

"F… yourself," snapped Boris.

"Feisty," said Parnell. "We've been tracking you for a number of years. You're sort of an office joke – the spy without a country. So, who are you working for now?"

Parnell kept at him for over an hour. But Boris, had to give him credit, never cracked. If anything, he became more feisty.

"You know we've tied you to three murders. Your man Michael will testify that you pulled the trigger."

"Michael, who? Don't know any Michaels, said Boris.

"Interesting, you've been paying someone you don't know?" quipped Parnell. "And the old man you shot on the Indian Reservation, we have an independent witness."

Parnell called in the guard and had Boris taken to his cell.

"I'd like to know what he was doing in Mexico," said Parnell, and as an afterthought, "I'm headed over to Holloman AFB. My ride is waiting for me. Want to come along?"

22   Showdown

The helicopter flight from Fort Huachuca to Holloman AFB was uneventful. We left Boris at the Fort Huachuca holding facility; he would later be transferred to a federal facility on the East Coast.

Earlier, Parnell contacted Colonel McElroy requesting that he, his aide, Major Dickerson, Dan Holuk, and, as a courtesy, Captain Bigalow be assembled. He did not mention that Boris had been captured or even hint at the financial probes he had initiated. The pretense for the meeting was ATF's interest in, and the future of, the Buck Rodgers Rifle.

McElroy arranged transportation to meet us at the helipad and take us to the secure conference room he had made available.

Captain Bigalow was there to greet me. "Shariff Barlow, you do get around," he said with some irritation.

"Agent Parnell," said Dan Holuk, "where is my prototype and what is going to happen to it?"

"Mr. Holuk, someone from the ATF will be contacting you. I understand they have already interviewed Dr. Borman and that Colt is interested in licensing your invention."

Colonel McElroy interrupted, "That's all well and good, but the Department of Defense will have to signoff on that. We don't want this technology to fall into the wrong hands."

"And speaking of wrong hands," said Parnell as he looked over at the two army officers, "We've captured the person who has been trying to get the new rifle. As you know, his efforts resulted in Dan's friend being killed. It's alleged he also killed the two men who took Nick's car containing the rifle. And, we have independent eyewitnesses to his killing of Mr. Night Owl on the reservation."

"Boris is an old Soviet spy, a spy without a country at this point, who now freelances for anyone who pays him. We think he was contracted by the Chinese to get the prototype. He employed the two car thieves and then killed them when they failed. Perhaps he would have killed them anyway."

"He had two other trusted henchmen whom he sent after Jimmy Crow once it was determined that Jimmy had the rifle."

"My question is, who told Boris that Jimmy had the rifle? I believe it was someone in this room," said Agent Parnell, looking from face to face.

Bigalow jumped to his feet, "I'm not going to sit here and let you imply me, or my men, of consorting with a spy!"

"No, no, sit back down and hear me out," said Parnell.

"We captured one of Boris's henchmen, Michael. He was reluctant to talk until Uncle Nakai, Jimmy Crow's Uncle, took him to the Navajo 'Truth Tree.' He later willingly talked, implicating Boris from start to finish. He told us Boris's information source was here at Holloman AF."

Colonel McElroy's expression was stoic as Parnell unraveled his tale. Major Dickerson, on the other hand, appeared to be getting agitated.

23 Flight

"Agent Parnell, this is all very interesting," said McElroy, "but if you could excuse me for a few minutes, I had some tocos last night that keep haunting me, Montezuma's revenge. I need to visit the men's room."

"By all means. Corporal, please accompany the Colonel."

The corporal was one of the two Air Force military police officers Parnell had requested to secure the meeting. The 'corporal' was, in fact, an airman first class with two stripes; his sergeant nodded his permission.

The two had been out of the room for fifteen minutes when the airman burst back in excitedly stating, "He's gone!!!"

"What do you mean he's gone?" Parnell yelled as he quickly headed to the restroom with me on his heels.

In the men's room, we found it had two entrances. One served the main hallway where we were, and the second served the offices in the back of the building. The hallway in the back emptied out into the rear parking lot. The parking space identified as Colonel McElroy's was empty.

Rushing back to the conference room, Parnell directed the sergeant to call base security to request a lockdown. It took ten minutes to get the right person with the authority to do so on the line, and another five for Parnell to identify himself and explain the need.

"Shit," he said to no one in particular, "McElroy is probably off base by now and headed to who knows where."

***

McElroy, suspecting where Parnell was going with his narrative, decided it was time to disappear.

Early in his career, he had met Boris in Germany. At the time, he was in charge of the platoon assigned to man Checkpoint Charlie. He was a Lieutenant, on the cusp of promotion to captain.

The problem, he and his wife enjoyed a lifestyle not supported on a company officer's pay. His wife, Mary Fine Fether, an enchanting Navajo girl whom he met during his initial duty assignment at Fort Huachuca, enjoyed visiting all the party spots in Europe, often on her own. As Mary's gambling debts became unmanageable, Boris saw an opportunity; he offered to cover them. McElroy slowly became ensnared in Boris's schemes, allowing contraband to flow through the checkpoint.

Over the years, McElroy's dealings with Boris became more commercial, dealing in America's secrets. By the time McElroy attained the rank of Colonel, he and Boris had become partners.

McElroy knew it was only a matter of time before the FBI traced the money trail back to him, if they had not already. When Parnell asked him to secure a meeting space, McElroy chose this building, knowing the restroom had two entrances. His car was parked in the back, just like any other workday.

He left the restroom via the second door, exited the building, and was out the base's back gate before Parnell missed him. He knew this day was coming and had prepared for it. A run to the Mexican border was out of the question. He knew the State Police would be watching for his car. He had an old 'beater' registered under an alias, prepositioned off base, containing escape essentials.

His wife, Mary Fine Fether, inherited her father's hunting cabin. As an Anglo, he could not own property in the Navajo Nation. Mary had passed away years earlier, so he kept the cabin in her name. Over the years, he became known as the old white man who occasionally visited the cabin. The few neighbors paid him no mind.

Colonel McElroy's challenge was the 250-mile drive to the cabin.

23 Hideaway

Parnell was livid, but there was nothing he could do.

"Major Dickerson, do you have any idea where McElroy might go?"

"No."

Parnell followed with a series of questions, many of which he already knew the answer to, but it helped to clear his mind.

Is he married? He's a widower. His wife was an Indian.
What kind of car does he have? An Audi A-10.
Where does he live? Cactus Bush Apartments.
Any siblings? He's an only child.
Parents? Dead.
Does he own any property he can go to? No.

Catching his breath, Parnell turned to Captain Bigalow. "Alert the State Police to be on the lookout for Colonel McElroy. He has probably ditched his car by now. Base Security should be able to give you a current picture of him."

"Captain, I also need you to get me a search warrant for his apartment. James and I are headed over there now."

"It's going to take me several hours to get that warrant," said Bigalow.

"That's okay," said Parnell as we left the room. "I don't think the Colonel will complain."

Colonel McElroy had a small townhouse on Spike Drive. As we were about to knock, his neighbor, an elderly lady, stepped out onto her porch. "William is not home; he parks his car there," she said, pointing to an empty space on the street.

"We know," said Parnell, "he asked us to pick something up for him. He's attending an important meeting and can't get away. And, dammit, please excuse my language, in the rush, he forgot to give me his key."

She stepped back a little, gave us both a good lookover, and said, "You look like nice young men. I have a spare key he asked me to hold for him for moments like this. Just a minute, let me get it."

I searched upstairs, two bedrooms and a bath, while Parnell took the first floor. The only thing I found was a framed photo of a woman in Indian garb, Navajo, if I wasn't mistaken. On the back was a label, *White Feather – 1994.*

Downstairs, Parnell had a bit of luck. He found an unopened envelope from the Navajo Nation Tax Authority in Window Rock, Arizona.

"You know it's a crime to open someone else's mail?" I said as Parnell, using a letter opener he found on the desk, slit the seal.

Taking out the single page, he read it and then handed it to me. "Looks like an annual tax assessment for a cabin in the Navajo Nation."

"He can't own property there," I said.

"Look who is listed as the owner."

I looked; it was White Feather. Apparently, he had kept the property in her name.

"It doesn't say where the cabin is; we need to go to Window Rock. You know some people up there?"

Looking at my watch, "If we leave now, we might get there before the tax assessment office closes."

We made it with minutes to spare. The clerk was not impressed with Parnell's FBI badge and started to tell us to come back in the morning. I laid my Navajo Nation Deputy Sheriff credentials on her and suggested that the council of elders would be calling her if she didn't cooperate.

It took her ten minutes to find the cabin. It was by Long Lake, just off Indian Service Road 30. "It's rather desolate up there," she said. "The property records have a small map attached showing the cabins' location. I'll make a copy for you."

"One more stop," I told Parnell, "the Public Safety Division."

We found the Division Head, Bud Evans, in his office.

Knocking on the door frame, I led Parnell into Bud's small office. "Great Bear, this is Agent Parnell. He's with the FBI. You remember that problem I told you about last time I was here? Well, this is more of it, and if we are lucky, the end of it."

I went on to give him details of the case, finishing up with, "We believe Colonel McElroy is holed up in an old hunting cabin by Long Lake. Agent Parnell has requested an FBI swat squad to assist us."

I could see that Evans was getting a little steamed about being left out.

"We need you and some of your men to assist in the takedown. There is a nearby community, Crystal, I think, where we will assemble our team early Tuesday morning in two days. Can you join us?"

"Yes," said a beaming Department Head. Pulling out a Reservation map and pointing to Long Lake, he suggested we use the Narbona Pass Picnic Area as a staging area. "It's closer to the target. Only five miles or so on back roads."

As we were walking out, Parnell grabbed my arm, "What was that all about?"

97

"You need the Res police to back you up. One, if McElroy runs, we'll need trackers. And two, I just bought you so much goodwill you can bottle it."

24 Last Act

'O dark thirty Tuesday morning, the FBI SWAT team, a team of five, arrived at the Narbona Pass Picnic Area. There were three pickup trucks with Navajo Police stenciled on their sides, one had a horse trailer; two horses inside. Parnell and I arrived with the SWAT team.

Parnell looked at the horse trailer and then at Chief Evans. "If he runs, we want to track him down," the Chief said.

Looking around, all Parnell saw were rolling hills with scrub pines.

Evans went on, "The land closer to the lake has several valleys, a small cliff line, and numerous places to hide. Your best bet is to catch him at the cabin."

"That's our plan. I think we're ready to go," said Parnell. "Chief, have your man take the lead. He knows the road, but he is not to engage. Tell him to pull up short of the cabin. My men will go in from there on foot."

We all suited up with bulletproof vests and clambered into assigned vehicles. The six vehicles started the slow drive down Service Road 30 toward White Feather's cabin.

***

McElroy, always one to get up early, was sitting on the porch when a flash of reflected light caught his attention. From his vantage point, he could see segments of the Service Road as it skirted a hill two or so miles away.

His first thought was, '*Shit, they found me.*' But not to panic, it might not be anything more than the road maintenance crew.

There was some work going on further up the road, where it had washed out after the last storm. But just to be safe, he went into the cabin, grabbed his rifle, and a few essentials. The rifle he used for hunting was a Savage Model 99 chambered for .30-30 cartridges. He was proficient with it.

McElroy moved two hundred yards up the slope and found a good spot among the boulders. He was well concealed with the sun to his back.

***

The lead vehicle stopped. Parnell and his men got and formed a semicircle around him. He directed the two sharpshooters to take up positions looking down on the cabin. The Navajo Police were to stay in the back – out of the way. Parnell led the remainder of his men down the drive toward the cabin. I was in the vanguard.

The cabin door was unlocked; Parnell and I entered.

"The coffee pot is still hot; McElroy must be around here somewhere." Stepping out the door, Parnell started to tell his men to search the area when the first shot rang out. Parnell was down. Subsequent shots pinned down his team.

Parnell was lying by the door. I grabbed his shoulders and dragged him back into the cabin. The bullet had missed his vest but hit his shoulder, probably shattering his shoulder socket. I got the vest off of him and applied pressure to the wound to stop the flow of blood.

At the sound of the first shot, Chief Evans ordered his men down the hill to secure the perimeter. One of the men, a seasoned scout, found McElroy's perch and three spent casings. McElroy was long gone.

One of the Chief's men was a former army medic. He took charge of Parnell, got a field dressing on him, and called for an ambulance.

"My tracker will find your man," said the Chief as he had the two horses brought down.

"I'm going with them," I said.

Grinning Evans said, "I thought as much. Can you still ride a horse?"

I got into the saddle without embarrassing myself, and the two of us were off. The 'tracker,' Tommy Light Foot, took the lead. We started from McElroy's nest. The initial trail was easy; McElroy was running and left deep footprints. He appeared to have slowed down after a quarter mile; the trail became more difficult to follow.

The landscape was mostly scrub pine, providing few places for concealment. There were several rock outcrops that we approached with some care.

Light Foot was able to lift the tiniest fragment of McElroy's flight: broken twigs, bent grass, a disturbed rock. Two miles further down the lake, which was a couple of hundred yards to our right, the ground changed to bedrock and rose up a hundred feet or so above the lake's shoreline.

As we approached a fissure in the cliff line, Tommy motioned for us to stop and pointed to the birds that were emerging from the fissure. "He's in there."

I dismounted and pulled the rifle from the saddle. It was a WWII .30 caliber carbine. I hoped the magazine had bullets. I chambered a round and called out, "McElroy, give up. Make it easy on all of us.

"This is the easy part," he yelled back, as he stepped out and, walking toward us along the cliff line, started firing at us. The lever action of his rifle allowed him to maintain a rate of fire that kept us pinned down. I let loose a couple of shots that chipped the stone to his right. He stepped onto a loose stone, causing him to slip, more accurately, to slip over the cliff's edge.

Tommy and I made our way down the body. It was a small drop, but sufficient to break a neck.

We lifted the body and placed it across the saddle of my horse. Leading the horse, I followed Tommy as we went back to the main group.

By the time we got there, Parnell had been treated by the paramedics and taken to the reservation's hospital.

"How is he?" I asked.

"The paramedics said he would live, but the shoulder joint would be a problem. He might lose the use of that arm," answered Evans.

Looking at the body lying across the horse, the Chief said, "You didn't tell me this was a *Dead or Alive* takedown."

25 Epilogue

Three weeks later, I was visiting Parnell. He had been moved to Johns Hopkins Hospital in Baltimore. The surgeons were reconstructing his shoulder joint, or more accurately, as he told me, the glenohumeral joint. McElroy's bullet had shattered the old joint. Parnell was the recipient of a new stainless-steel joint.

"My first step in becoming the bionic man," he joked. "The Doc's promised me I should be 80 percent back to normal in three months. But golf might be a problem."

"Thanks for coming to see me. I understand McElroy is dead – broken neck?"

"Actually, the Bureau brought me to DC to fill in some details. I understand Boris is being held at the Petersburg Federal Prison. The Justice Department wants to keep him close by as they decide what to do with him."

"One of their lawyers, a young guy who talks too much, interviewed me last week," said Parnell. "I think I learned more from him than he got from me. He provided a nice summary of Boris the spy."

"As we already knew, Boris was a Soviet spy. When the Soviet Union collapsed in '91, he worked for the GRU for a number of years until a falling out. He retired for a year or so, enjoying the sunny beaches of Florida."

"Boris got back into the game when he met Jeffry Epstein in the late '90s, becoming Epstein's concierge at his waterfront estate in Florida. The two quickly developed a friendship that opened doors for Boris. It wasn't long after that that he started assisting with the 'Lolita Express.'

"In this new environment, he realized he had access to all kinds of state and personal secrets, which he was able to capitalize on. Then it all collapsed when Epstein was arrested."

"Boris took a step back from the world stage. He put on weight and grew a mustache, giving him the look we all know today. But he liked the excitement espionage provided. So, he took on small novelty cases like obtaining experimental weapons, Buck Rogers-type weapons, for the Chinese. They provided basic information as to *where*. He was to provide the *when* and *how*. The Chinese weren't paying that much; Boris just liked the chase. And that brought us to Dark Valley."

"And now, New Mexico wants to try him for murder. It must be nice to be wanted by so many," I said. "Did we ever figure out why he was in Mexico?"

"Yes, the Chinese wanted to get him out of the country before he blew their assets. The cartel was one stop in their distribution chain. He was to be flown out of the country at the end of the week. The raid derailed that."

"Now, why are you really here?"

"Your boss, Oscar Vicente, offered me a job. He was impressed with my handling of the Susan Dillingham case last year and with my involvement with the current case. He wants me to become a G-man. He'll bring me in as a senior Special Agent with the expectation of promotion to Supervisory Special Agent within twelve months. He did mention the need to attend some courses at Quantico to absorb the Bureau's culture."

"Now, why would you do that. You have a nice, quiet life as an Arizona Sheriff."

"I would question the quiet part, but I'm thinking I'd like something with more career potential. I need to talk it over with my wife before giving him an answer."

End